Little White Puffy Cloud

One day in Teletubbyland, the Teletubbies were watching the clouds.
A big fluffy cloud floated by.

Big fluffy cloud!

A long thin wispy cloud floated by.

Long thin wispy cloud!

A little white puffy cloud floated by.

Little white puffy cloud!

And do you know what happened?

No!

The little white puffy cloud floated ...

INDOORS!

Uh-oh!
Little white puffy cloud indoors!

The Teletubbies followed the cloud indoors.
It was time for tubby custard.

But the Teletubbies found it a little inconvenient having a cloud indoors ...

and Laa-Laa spilt her tubby custard.

splosh

Along came the Noo-noo.

The Noo-noo tidied up the tubby custard.

sucky sucky sluuurrrp

Then the Noo-noo tidied up the cloud.

Thank you,
Noo-noo!

sucky

sluuuurp

But all that tubby custard and all that cloud got very mixed up inside the Noo-noo...

The little white puffy cloud had turned pink!

Bye-bye, special pink tubby custard cloud.

Bye-bye!

Teletubbies love the special pink tubby custard cloud.
And Teletubbies love each other very much!

Big Hug!

Dipsy and the Decoration

One day in Teletubbyland, something appeared from far away.

What a pretty thing!

It was a decoration.

The decoration decorated the tree.

Then, the decoration disappeared.

ping!

The decoration decorated the house.

Then, the
decoration
disappeared.

Look!

How decorative!

Then, the
decoration
disappeared.

Then, the decoration disappeared.

How decorative!

How decorative!

Along came Dipsy.

Then, the decoration disappeared.

Where had the
decoration gone?

Decoration!
Decoration!

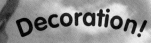

Decoration!

Look at that! The decoration had decorated Dipsy!

Decoration
decorated
Dipsy!

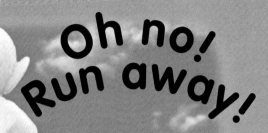

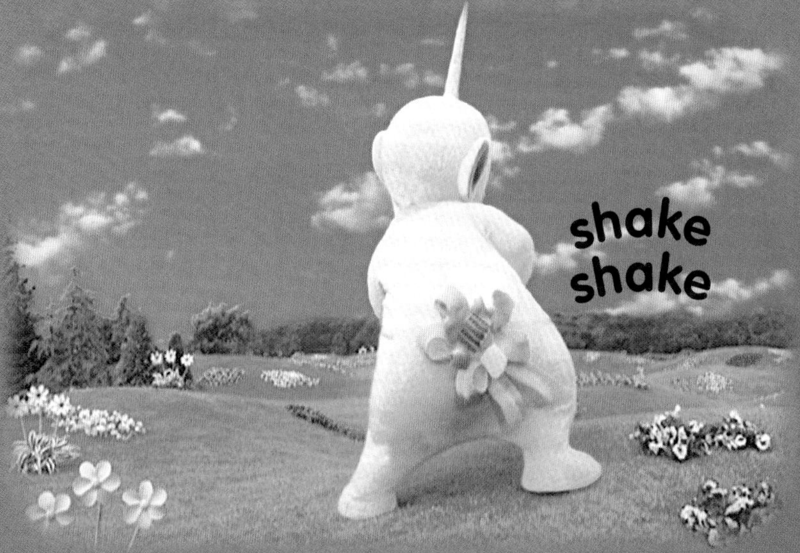
shake
shake

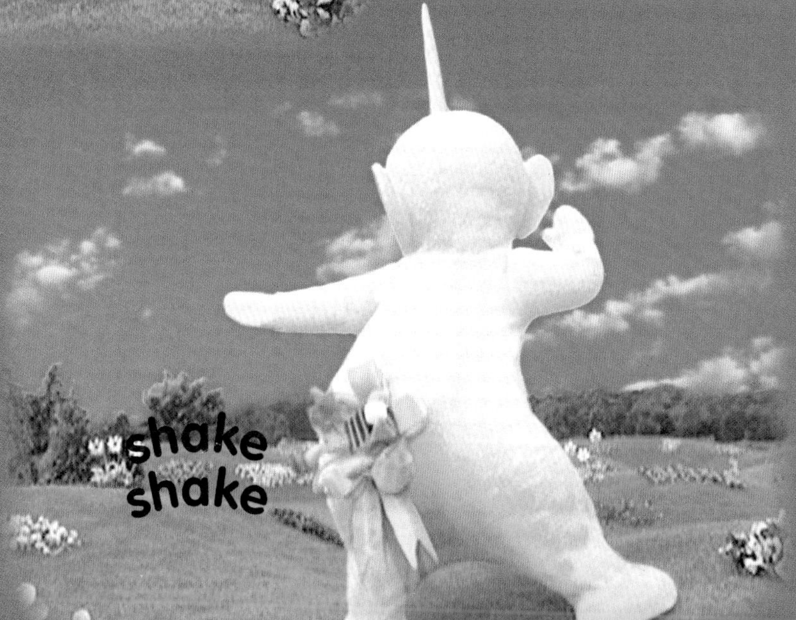
shake
shake

And then the decoration disappeared.

All gone!

ping!

Teletubbies love each other very much.

Big Hug!

Original paperback editions of Little White Puffy Cloud and Dipsy and the Decoration
first published in 2000 and 1999 by BBC Worldwide Limited
Woodlands, 80 Wood Lane, London W12 0TT
This hardback edition © BBC Worldwide Limited 2002
From original TV scripts by Andrew Davenport
Digiframes™ by Screenscene Limited
Designed by The Dirty Cat Company Design Partnership
Text, design and illustrations © BBC Worldwide Limited 2002
Teletubbies characters and logo © and ™ 1996 Ragdoll Limited
Printed and bound in Singapore

ISBN 0 563 47649 4